Sparkleton

The Magic Day

READ MORE SPARKLETON BOOKS!

1

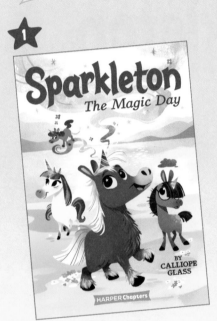

2

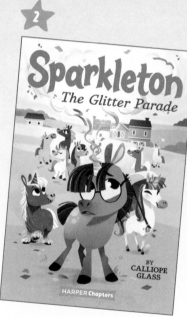

Sparkleton
The Magic Day

BY CALLIOPE GLASS

ILLUSTRATED BY
HOLLIE MENGERT

HARPER **Chapters**

An Imprint of HarperCollinsPublishers

To Goodyear,

the laziest horse I ever loved.

Sparkleton #1: The Magic Day

Copyright © 2020 by HarperCollins Publishers

All rights reserved. Printed in Canada.

www.harperchapters.com

Library of Congress Control Number: 2019950248

ISBN 978-0-06-294792-5 — ISBN 978-0-06-294791-8 (pbk.)

The artist used Photoshop to create the digital illustrations for this book.

Typography by Andrea Vandergrift

20 21 22 TC 10 9 8 7 6 5

❖

First Edition

TABLE OF CONTENTS

1

Magic Should Not Be Boring

"**T**his is boring," Sparkleton said. He slammed the book shut with one hoof. "Magic should not be boring."

Sparkleton was a unicorn.

Sparkleton didn't have his magic yet. But he still had to learn everything *about* magic. All the young unicorns in Shimmer Lake did. Gramma Una said it was so they'd be ready when their magic came.

SPARKLETON

Small

Purple

Doesn't have magic yet

LOVES magic

HATES rules

Shaggy

Especially hates rules ABOUT magic

Sparkleton didn't mind learning about magic. He *loved* magic! But he did mind being *bored*.

"I can't wait until I get my magic," Sparkleton told his sister, Nella. "I'm going to grant everybody's wishes. It's going to be glitterrific!"

Nella rolled her eyes at him. She was practicing nearby. She traced figure eights in the air with her horn.

"You don't even know if you're going to *get* wish-granting magic like me and Gramma," Nella pointed out. "You could end up with confetti magic, or healing magic, or even cleaning magic. You never know."

"Blech!" Sparkleton said. He stamped one hoof. Wish-granting magic is the *best*, and I love it. I *know* I'll get it. And I'll be so *happy*!"

He galloped in a little circle, he was so excited.

NELLA

Has wish-granting magic

Very long black mane (she's vain about it, too)

Blue coat

Super-duper annoying

Ticklish right here

Loves rules (See? Told you she was annoying)

Nella stopped practicing and looked right at Sparkleton. "*You'll* be happy, huh? What about your friends?" she asked. "Magic is all about making *others* happy."

Sparkleton thought for a moment. She had a point.

"I know!" he said. "I'll give Gabe wings so he can pick us the best apples from the top of the tree!" Gabe would like flying. And Sparkleton would like the apples! It was a win-win.

Nella snorted and tossed her glossy black mane. "Gabe is afraid of heights. He'd hate flying! It's a good thing you can't grant wishes," she said. "You're not responsible enough."

That gave Sparkleton a great idea. An *incredible* idea. A *sparkletastic* idea.

"I'll prove that I can be a good wish-granting unicorn!" Sparkleton said. He jumped up and down.

"How?" Nella said.

"I'll make a wish!" Sparkleton shouted.

You read one chapter. Off to a GLITTERRIFIC start!

2

This Is a Terrible Idea

"I'll wish for wish-granting magic!" Sparkleton said. "And you can grant it with *your* wish-granting magic!"

"That's against the rules," Nella said. She looked shocked. "I'm not allowed to just grant someone magical powers. We'd be breaking like six different rules!"

Sparkleton shrugged. "When has that stopped you before?" he asked.

"Every single time!" Nella shot back. "I *never* break the rules."

This was true. Nella was a boring Goody Two-horseshoes.

Nella shook her head. "For the record, this is a terrible idea."

Sparkleton sprang up. His heart was pounding with excitement. "Does that mean you'll do it?"

Nella sighed.

"Yes," she said. "But just for one day." Nella nudged Sparkleton with her nose. "You're my little brother and I want you to be happy."

"You do?" Sparkleton could hardly believe his luck.

"Sure," Nella said. She blew a puff of warm air in Sparkleton's face. "But if Gramma Una ever finds out about this, I'll give you the unicorn pox and make you very itchy for the rest of your life."

That sounded more like Nella.

She blew her mane away from her face and began the spell.

First, she stamped her front hooves.

Then she lowered her nose to the ground and snorted three times.

Finally, she traced a figure eight in the air with the tip of her horn. It began to glow. Nella looked deep into Sparkleton's eyes. He stared back at her. For a long moment, neither of them blinked. Then—

"Thy wish is granted," Nella said. She tapped Sparkleton on the nose with her horn.

A tingle ran from the tip of Sparkleton's nose all the way to the bottoms of his back hooves.

Sparkleton had seen Nella and Gramma Una do the wish-granting spell a million times.

But he'd never had it done to *him*!

You read two chapters!
Are you feeling SPARKLETASTIC?

★ 2 ☆☆☆☆☆☆☆☆☆☆

3

It's the Most Amazing Thing

"I feel different," Sparkleton said.

His body felt just the same. His hooves were still his hooves. His ears were still his ears. Even his horn felt the same.

But somewhere near his heart, there was a little bright feeling. It hadn't been there before. And he knew exactly what it was.

Magic.

"Finally!" Sparkleton yelled.

A few sparks flew out of his horn. He could hardly wait to get started.

"Make a wish!" he said to Nella. "Wish for anything! No, wait, wish for a chocolate cake. No, wait, wish for *ten* chocolate cakes."

Nella shook her head. "You're already doing it wrong," she said. "This is going to go very badly. I can tell."

"Wish for me to have gold hooves!" he said. Sparkleton had always wanted gold hooves.

"I'm not wishing for anything from you," Nella said. "And I don't want to be anywhere near you when somebody does make a wish."

She turned her nose up and trotted away. Sparkleton didn't care. He had big plans.

"What *fun*!" Sparkleton shouted just to hear his voice echo through the forest.

"What is?" a voice asked.

Sparkleton jumped straight into the air.

A white unicorn trotted into Sparkleton's glen. It was Willow, one of his two best friends.

WILLOW

Giant brain for big plans

Turquoise mane

Has over 30 mottos

HATES bug bites

Never met a bad idea she didn't LOVE

"Willow!" Sparkleton said, prancing with excitement. "Willow, it's the most amazing thing!"

"Goblins are line-dancing on a rainbow made of magic gemstones?" Willow asked.

"What?" Sparkleton said. He was confused. Goblins?

"That was the most amazing thing I could think of," Willow explained.

Sparkleton shook his head. This was *way* more amazing than that.

"No," he said. "Nella gave me wish-granting magic until sunset!"

"Oh," Willow said. Her eyes went wide. "Oh, oh, oh! That really is the most amazing thing!" She danced around him in excitement. "It'll probably be a disaster. But what if it isn't?!"

That was one of Willow's favorite mottos. She had a bunch of them.

"We're going to have so much *fun*, Sparkleton!" she went on.

"I know!" Sparkleton said. "I can't wait to get started! Make a wish!"

"Hmm," Willow said. She stopped dancing. "You know how to grant wishes, right?"

"How hard can it be?" Sparkleton asked. "I've seen Nella and Gramma Una do the spell about eighty million times."

"Okay!" Willow said. She still looked very excited, but she also still wasn't making a wish. "This is *awesome* and I am *super* happy for you," she went on, "but I don't think I . . . *deserve* to be the very first wisher. Let's go find Gabe!" Gabe was Willow's and Sparkleton's other best friend.

Sparkleton grinned. "Great idea," he said. "Gabe will *love* this!"

Willow shook her head. "No, he'll hate it . . ." she said. "But what if he doesn't?"

4

Let's Start with Something Small

Sparkleton and Willow galloped straight to Gabe's garden. They could see the other unicorns their age playing in the field nearby. But they didn't stop to say hi.

They were on a mission.

Gabe's garden was at the corner of the field. It wasn't most people's idea of a garden. There were no flowers. No stepping-stone paths. No herbs or vegetables.

GABE

LOVES mushrooms

Blue mood →

← HATES pretty much EVERYTHING else

Blue coat →

Unless mushrooms counted as vegetables.

Gabe's "garden" was actually a dark, damp cave full of mushrooms.

"Please be careful where you walk," Gabe told Sparkleton and Willow when they came into the cave. "Some of my mushrooms are very small and easy to—"

Squish.

Sparkleton lifted one hoof. A flattened mushroom was stuck to the bottom of it.

"Whoops," Sparkleton said. "Sorry. Hey, guess what?"

"Sparkleton's got wish-granting powers!" Willow said.

"Oh no," Gabe said. He took a step back.

"Oh, yes!" Sparkleton said. "I knew you'd be happy for me!"

Gabe looked at Sparkleton, then at Willow, then at Sparkleton again. "And I bet you want me to make a wish," he said.

"Right!" Sparkleton said.

"And I bet you haven't tried this out on anyone else yet," Gabe continued.

"Right!" Willow said. "Gabe, this is going to be so cool . . . If it isn't an utter catastrophe!"

"I don't know what that means," Gabe said.

"It means it's going to go super sparkly!" Sparkleton said. "Relax, I'm a natural!"

"You're just going to bug me until I say yes, aren't you?" Gabe asked.

"Uh-huh!" Sparkleton and Willow said together.

"Okay, fine," Gabe said. "I wish—"

"Wait!" Willow interrupted. "We should plan this first. Let's start with something small."

The three unicorns trooped out of the cave and into the field. Sparkleton looked around, thinking. The sun had gone behind a cloud. Shimmer Lake looked kind of . . . gray.

"Why don't you wish for the clouds to go away?" Sparkleton asked Gabe.

"Wow!" Willow said. "That is *really* not starting small. Clouds are part of *giant* weather

systems. If you mess with them, you could accidentally start a big storm . . . or a heat wave . . . or worse!"

That didn't sound good.

"So let's do it and see what happens!" Willow said. "It'll be like a *science experiment*."

Sparkleton and Willow grinned at each other. Sparkleton was glad he had such smart friends.

Gabe sighed. "Fine. I wish for the clouds to go away," he muttered unhappily.

Sparkleton took a deep breath. He'd been waiting for this moment his entire life. Granting wishes was going to be *so cool*.

First, he stamped his front hooves: left, then right.

Then he lowered his nose to the ground and snorted three times.

Finally, he traced a figure eight in the air with the tip of his horn. It began to glow.

Sparkleton was so excited he could hardly stand still. *I'm doing it!* he thought. *I'm really doing it!*

Thy wish is granted.

The little bright place near Sparkleton's heart got brighter, and he shivered. The magic was happening!

"Oh dear," Willow said. "Sparkleton, look!"

The sky above Shimmer Lake was still cloudy. But now there was another little cloud, hanging over Gabe's head like a cold, fluffy hat.

"You did it wrong," Sparkleton told Gabe.

"Hey!" Gabe said. "You're the one who granted the wish, Sparkleton."

"I know," Sparkleton said. "But I did the

spell just like Nella does it. Maybe you didn't *really* want the sun to come out."

Gabe glared at Sparkleton. His little cloud made a little grumble of thunder.

"Why would I wish for this?" asked Gabe.

"I'm sure it will go away soon," Willow told Gabe. "Or else it won't," she added.

"One or the other!" Sparkleton agreed.

Gabe shook his head hard. He was trying to knock the cloud away, but it stayed put. He galloped over to the edge of the clearing and back.

The cloud stayed right over his head the whole time.

"Great," Gabe said. "Just what I've always wanted."

"I'm glad you like it!" Sparkleton said. "Hey, let's go show the other unicorn foals!"

Sparkleton, Willow, and Gabe (and Gabe's little cloud) trotted over to their friends. They were playing unicorn tag in the meadow.

DALE
Likes: eating daisies
Hates: eating anything else

ROSIE
Likes: anything shiny
Hates: anything dirty

ZUZU
Likes: climbing things
Hates: weird smells

BRITTA
Likes: listening to ladybugs eat leaves
Hates: sleeping

"Hey!" Sparkleton called. "Look at Gabe's awesome cloud!"

"Whoa," Dale said softly.

"How did *that* happen?" Rosie asked.

"Can I touch it?" Zuzu asked. She trotted up and nosed Gabe's cloud. Then she sneezed.

"It's wet!" she said.

"It's a cloud," Gabe said. "It's made of water."

"I knew that," said Britta. "Where did it come from?"

29 ↻

Sparkleton couldn't keep quiet any longer.

Then another voice piped up from just over the hill.

"Hey, guys!"

A heart-spotted unicorn trotted over to them. Her hoofbeats sounded like bells ringing.

"Ugh," Sparkleton muttered. "Twinkle."

Sparkleton hated Twinkle. She was so *nice*.

TWINKLE

Rainbow horn (UGH!)

Smart and kind (whatever)

Rainbow mane (Double UGH!)

Good at school (annoying!!!!!!!!!!!!)

Tiny hooves (annoying)

"Hey, Twinkle!" Willow said. She swished her tail to wave hello. "Come see! Sparkleton has wish-granting magic for a whole day!"

"Stars!" Twinkle said, trotting over.

"Sparkleton, that's glitterrific! Granting a wish is the nicest thing a unicorn can do for someone!"

Sparkleton rolled his eyes.

"Sparkleton, will you grant my wish?" Zuzu asked. "I wish my mane was orange!"

"Zuzu asked first," Sparkleton said.

"Ready!" she said. She tossed her mane.

Sparkleton wiggled excitedly. Granting wishes made him feel great. He loved having magic!

He stamped his front hooves: left, then right. Then he snorted three times.

Finally, he traced a figure eight in the air.

Personally, I would have asked for a purple mane, he thought. *Oh well.*

"Thy wish is granted," he said. He tapped Zuzu on the nose with his glowing horn.

Zuzu's tail turned blue.

Five chapters down. You must be really FOCUSED!

6

Something Weird Is Going On

"**H**ey!" Zuzu said.

"I guess she wished wrong, too," Gabe said sourly. His cloud gave a tiny little rumble and started raining on his head.

"Super," he said.

"I didn't do anything wrong!" Zuzu said. She twisted her head around to look at her tail again.

"Hmm," Willow said. "I think something

weird is going on. Let's try again. Who else wants a wish granted?"

"Me!" Rosie yelled. "I wish there was a river of glitter right here so I could splash around in it!"

Sparkleton liked the sound of that.

"Concentrate on the idea of a river of glitter," Willow told Rosie. "Focus hard on it!"

Rosie squeezed her eyes shut.

"Glitterglitterglitterglitter," she muttered.

This is going to be so cool, Sparkleton thought. *I wonder if surfboards work on glitter rivers.*

There was only one way to find out.

Sparkleton did the spell.

He stomped his hooves. He waved his horn. The warm place next to his heart glowed.

"Thy wish is granted," he said, tapping Rosie on the nose.

Out of nowhere, a huge wave of mud slid across the meadow. It splashed over the young unicorns, coating them all in muck from head to toe.

Rosie started crying.

"Okay," Willow said, "I'm pretty sure that wasn't Rosie's fault." She shook her head and mud splattered on Gabe's face. Luckily, the little rain cloud washed it off.

"It was a good try, Sparkleton!" said Twinkle. "I'm sure you'll get it right next time!"

She bumped his shoulder in a friendly way.

Sparkleton glared at Twinkle. *Ugh, she's the worst.*

"Would you grant my wish?" Britta asked. "I've always wanted to fly!"

"You know," Gabe said, "I don't think this is a great—"

"Sure I can!" Sparkleton was already stomping his hooves. He was going to prove he could do this right!

Britta held her breath. The tips of her ears turned red while she waited.

I'm awesome at this, Sparkleton thought. He waved his horn in figure eights. *I don't get why unicorns have to wait so long to get their magic.*

"Thy wish is granted," Sparkleton said when the spell was done. Britta let her breath out with a whoosh.

Sparkleton tapped Britta on the nose with his horn. The little bright place near his heart got brighter, and he felt his new magic working.

"Yay!" Britta said. "I'm going to fly! I'm going to—"

All of a sudden, Britta fell right over. *Splat!* She landed in the mud.

"Help!" Britta said. "I can't get up!"

The unicorns all hurried over. Britta had become so heavy that she could barely lift her head.

"I can't stand up!" Britta said. "I'm stuck here!"

Sparkleton shook his head, confused. What the sparkle was happening?

7

Sparkleton, You're a Genius!

"**H**elp!" Britta said again. She tried to get up, but she couldn't get her legs under her. Instead of lifting her up, the spell was pulling her down!

The young unicorns stood around her helplessly.

"We don't know what to do," Dale said.

"We don't even know what's going wrong," Zuzu said.

"Maybe it's goblins," said Willow.

"It's opposites," Gabe said.

"It's an unsolved mystery," Rosie said. "You're stuck like that forever, Britta."

"It's opposites," Gabe said again.

"Wait," Sparkleton said. He had an amazing idea. "What if it's opposites?"

"I just said that," Gabe said.

"Sparkleton, you're a genius!" Willow cried.

"But I— Oh, never mind," Gabe said.

"Gabe wished for sunny skies, and instead, another cloud appeared," Willow explained to the others. "Zuzu wished for an orange mane, and then her tail turned blue."

"Blue is the opposite of orange," Sparkleton said. "And the tail is on the opposite end of a unicorn from the mane!"

Zuzu nodded. "And mud is the opposite of glitter!"

"And being too heavy is the opposite of flying!" said Sparkleton.

"So what do we do about Britta?" Dale asked.

Willow frowned. "If all the wishes Sparkleton grants come out opposite," she said, "then maybe if you wish for the opposite of what you want . . ."

"You'll get what you *actually* want!" Twinkle finished. "Brilliant, Willow!"

"Fine," Britta said. "I wish I was even heavier."

Sparkleton looked at Gabe and Willow. They looked back at him. Gabe sighed, and Willow shrugged.

MIGHT AS WELL TRY IT!

"Might as well try it" was another one of Willow's mottos.

Sparkleton did the spell. He touched Britta's nose with his horn. *This better work*, he thought. *I don't want to look like I don't know what I'm doing.*

A breathless moment passed.

And then Britta lifted her head up from the ground.

"It worked!" Sparkleton shouted. He did a little prance in place.

Britta climbed to her hooves.

"We did it!" Willow said. She knocked horns with Sparkleton in celebration.

Slowly but surely, Britta rose into the air.

"Uh-oh," Gabe said.

"No, wait," Sparkleton said. "This isn't—"

Britta rose higher and higher.

"Help!" Britta said. "I can't control it! I can't come down!"

A gentle breeze pushed Britta right into the branches of a big oak tree. Her mane and tail got tangled in the twigs, and soon she was completely stuck.

"Help!" Britta called.

Gabe tilted his head thoughtfully. "I guess floating away is actually the opposite of being even heavier," he said.

"But is being stuck in a tree better than being stuck on the ground?" Dale asked.

"No!" Britta yelled. "No, it is not!"

Willow frowned. "No matter what we do, the wishes come out opposite," she said. "The wishers can't be the problem.

So what's going wrong?"

"Sparkleton, how did you *get* this magic in the first place?" Rosie asked.

"Nella," Sparkleton said. Suddenly, it all made sense.

I bet she did this just to mess with me!

Twinkle shook her head. "I don't think that's possible," she said. "I think wish granting only works when you want to help the other person."

Sparkleton ignored her.

Brrrrrrring!

All the unicorns jumped.

"The lunch bell!" Willow said. Lunchtime in Shimmer Lake meant everyone had to go home to their families.

Sparkleton swallowed hard. He felt very nervous all of a sudden. Going home for lunch meant facing Nella . . . and *Gramma Una*!

Willow and Sparkleton looked at each other. *Uh-oh.*

8

It's a Good Thing
That Didn't Happen

When Sparkleton got back home, Nella and Gramma Una were already in the grassy field where they ate.

"Hello, kiddo," Gramma Una said, nuzzling Sparkleton's forehead.

Don't act suspicious, Sparkleton reminded himself. He didn't want Gramma Una to find out that he had magic.

"Hello!" Sparkleton said. "Everything's fine!

Nothing strange is happening today!"

Nella glared at Sparkleton and he stopped talking.

"Nella, how is your studying going?" Gramma Una asked her.

Nella cleared her throat nervously.

"Okay, I guess," she said. "I think I'll be ready for my first trip to the human world soon. I can hardly wait to grant a wish there!"

GRAMMA UNA

Loves terrible jokes

Has wish-granting magic

Knows everything

Silver mane

White coat

Silver tail

Old. Really old. Super-duper old. (Never tell her that to her face)

"Be patient, Nella," Gramma Una said. "Remember, the most important thing isn't *when* you grant a wish—"

"It's *how* you grant it," Nella finished.

The unicorns ate in silence for a little while. Then Gramma Una turned to Sparkleton. "Sparkleton, you aren't usually so quiet."

Sparkleton's mouthful of grass got stuck in his throat. He coughed.

"Is everything okay?" Gramma Una asked.

"Uh," Sparkleton said. He cleared his throat. "I was just thinking . . ." Sparkleton wondered if there was a way for him to ask Gramma Una's advice without telling her what had happened.

"Gramma," Sparkleton said, "I have a question. About . . . something that hasn't actually happened."

"I see," Gramma Una said.

"Imagine that a young unicorn got wish-granting magic for one day," Sparkleton said. "But all the wishes he granted came out opposite."

Gramma Una nodded seriously. "I'm imagining it," she said.

"So," Sparkleton continued. "Why did that happen? Was it because his sister messed up the spell when she gave him wish-granting powers?"

"Hey!" Nella said. She poked Sparkleton with her horn.

"Oh no," Gramma Una said. "Your sister—I mean, this imaginary sister—didn't mess up the spell. This imaginary sister knows that spell backward and forward." Then Gramma frowned. "She also knows she isn't supposed to use it that way."

Nella flicked her ears nervously.

"Anyway," Gramma Una said, "it's a good thing that didn't happen, because if it *did*, it would be very bad."

Sparkleton's eyes got wide. "Bad *how*?" he asked.

"When the young unicorn's wish-granting magic wore off at the end of the day," Gramma went on, "all those opposite wishes would become permanent!"

"Permanent?" Sparkleton squeaked.

"That's right, kiddo," Gramma Una said. "All of his friends would be stuck with rain clouds over their heads *forever*."

Uh-oh! How do you think I'll **SOLVE** this problem?

★ ★ ★ ★ ★ ★ ★ ★ 8 ☆ ☆ ☆ ☆

9

This Better Not Go Horribly Wrong

After lunch, Sparkleton told his friends about Gramma Una's warning. "Then she said only the unicorn who granted the wishes can undo them." Everyone started talking at once.

Gramma Una really does know EVERYTHING.

Britta's stuck up there FOREVER?

"But Gramma Una is a legend!" Twinkle said. "All the wish granters in my family ask her for advice all the time!"

Sparkleton rolled his eyes. Twinkle was always talking about how there were wish granters in her family.

"Let's give it another shot," Willow said. "Let's try more opposite wishes."

"It will probably end in disaster," said Rosie.

"But what if it doesn't?" Willow said.

Willow trotted over to Zuzu.

"Zuzu," Willow said, "your tail used to be black, right? So maybe you have to wish for the opposite of a black tail."

"A white mane," Gabe said.

"Okay," Zuzu said, "I wish I had a white mane."

Sparkleton stamped his hooves and waved his horn.

Here goes, he thought. *I hope this works.* So far granting wishes had been no fun at all.

But when the spell was done, Zuzu's tail was still blue . . . and her mane was still striped.

Sparkleton shook his head, disappointed. His forelock brushed across his eyes.

His white forelock.

Uh-oh.

Sparkleton looked around.

"*Everyone's* mane turned white!" Twinkle said.

"Except mine," Zuzu pointed out.

"Oh dear," Willow said. "This time, 'opposite' meant that everyone got the wish granted *except* the wisher."

"Gah!" Sparkleton said. He stomped one hoof.

"So now everyone in Shimmer Lake has a white mane," Zuzu said.

"And I'm stuck in a tree!" Britta added.

"And I still have a cloud over my head," Gabe finished.

Hmm.

"Well," Sparkleton said to Gabe, "*that* one should be easy to fix."

"Oh, really?" Gabe said. He did not look hopeful. Sparkleton wasn't bothered by it. Gabe was always gloomy about everything. That's why he was friends with Sparkleton— so Sparkleton could cheer him up!

"What you want is *no cloud over your head*, right?" Sparkleton asked.

"Right," Gabe agreed.

"So what's the opposite of no cloud over your head?" Sparkleton asked.

Gabe thought hard.

"A cloud over my head?" he said.

"Yes!" Sparkleton cried. "All you need to do is wish for a cloud over your head!"

"This better not go horribly wrong," Gabe said.

"Don't worry," Willow told him. "Even if it does, it will probably be really cool."

Gabe sighed.

"I wish for a cloud over my head," he said obediently.

Sparkleton performed the spell.

A cloud appeared *under* Gabe's head.

"See?" Willow said cheerfully. "It *did* go horribly wrong, and it *is* really cool!"

The top cloud began to snow. Sparkleton watched as the snow piled up on Gabe's forehead until his entire head was covered in cold white fluff.

"You're right, Willow," Sparkleton said. "That is *really cool*."

Gabe sneezed miserably. The snow scattered.

A tiny tornado began spinning near his left nostril. Gabe sneezed again.

My head is the cheese in a cloud sandwich.

And I HATE cheese.

"Okay," Willow said. "I guess the opposite wishes just don't work."

"So what do we do now?" Gabe said. A tiny bolt of lightning zapped his ear. "Ouch!" He jumped.

Sparkleton looked at the sky. The sun was getting close to the horizon. There wasn't much time left.

"I have an idea," Willow said. She smiled at Sparkleton. "And it's terrible."

10

Go Big or Go Home

As the sun moved toward the horizon, Willow paced back and forth. "I heard about some goblin magic that might work," she said.

Everyone gasped.

"Goblin magic isn't very . . . *safe*," Twinkle said.

Willow flicked her tail. "You know my motto," she said.

"'Safe, schmafe!'" Sparkleton and Gabe said.

Willow had a lot of mottos, but that one was Sparkleton's favorite.

"No," Willow said. "The *other* one."

"'Let's get risky'?" Sparkleton asked. That one was good, too.

"No," Willow said, "the other other one."

"'Go big or go home'?" Gabe asked.

"Yep," Willow said. "*That* one. Now, first we need to get Britta down here."

"How are you going to do that?" Britta asked.

"I have a plan," Willow said.

"Is it safe?" Zuzu asked.

"Of course not," Willow said. She looked a little offended.

Soon Zuzu was standing on Gabe's back, and Gabe was standing on Twinkle's back. All the unicorns were piled up, except Willow, who was standing nearby. She held a rope in her teeth.

The whole tower of unicorns wobbled.

Sparkleton grinned. This was *awesome*.

"This really *isn't* safe," Zuzu said. She looked down at the ground nervously.

"Nope!" Willow agreed. "Now, Zuzu, I want you to reach out *very carefully*—"

"Sparkleton!" cried an angry voice from across the field. "What in the name of all that glitters is going on?"

Sparkleton whipped his head around. The tower of unicorns teetered.

Nella was cantering toward them. Her long mane was white and her eyes flashed. She looked very, very angry.

"Oh, hey, Nella," Sparkleton said. "How's it going?"

"My mane is *white* and your friends are all *standing* on each other, Sparkleton," Nella said. "That's how it's going."

She looked around. "What's with all this mud? Why is Britta in a tree? What happened to Gabe's head? What have you been *doing*?"

Sparkleton winced.

"Well . . ." he said. He took a deep breath, and then started talking fast.

Every wish I grant turns out opposite! We tried to fix it by making **OPPOSITE** opposite wishes. But we ended up in even **BIGGER** trouble. And Gramma says everything's **PERMANENT** once the sun goes down. And the sun is about to go down! So we're trying **GOBLIN MAGIC**. Because we're almost out of time, and **WE DON'T KNOW WHAT ELSE TO DO!**

He gasped for air.

Nella frowned. "But Gramma didn't say to use goblin magic," she said.

"No," Sparkleton agreed. "She said I have to figure out what I'm doing wrong, and undo it myself. But that's going to take forever, and we don't have forever."

"Yeah, but you know my motto," Nella said.

Nella has a motto?

"Yeah," Sparkleton said. "'Goblin magic is never the answer.'"

"That's right," Nella said.

"I could have told you *that*," Gabe muttered.

"You got us into this, Sparkleton," Nella said. She looked him dead in the eye. He gulped nervously. "Now get us out of it. Without goblin magic. *Before sunset.*"

11

Thank You,
Little Brother

Sparkleton looked at the sky. The clouds were turning pink, and the sun was getting close to setting. There was almost no time left. He stamped his hoof nervously.

"So, okay. What do we know?" he said.

"Well, first of all," Nella said, "we know this isn't my fault."

Sparkleton rolled his eyes.

"And it's not the wisher's fault!" Zuzu said.

"That's true," Willow said. "I thought maybe the person making the wish had to think about their wish while they did it, or else it wouldn't work."

"But I was thinking about glitter the whole time," Rosie said. "And look at me!" She was still covered in mud from head to toe.

"And I was thinking—" Britta started, but Sparkleton interrupted her.

"*Wait a second*," he said. He was a genius. "That's it!"

Willow's eyes were wide. "What?"

"*Thinking*," Sparkleton said. "While I was doing the spell, I wasn't thinking about the unicorn who was *making* the wish!"

He turned to Nella. "Remember what Gramma said? 'We grant wishes to make people happy'!"

"Duh," Nella said. "Wait, are you telling me you've been thinking of yourself this whole time? Even when you were granting wishes? You have to focus on the wisher, Sparkleton! That's the first rule Gramma ever taught us."

Sparkleton shrugged. "You know how much I hate rules," he said.

Nella bonked her horn against a tree. She looked very frustrated.

"Anyway!" Sparkleton said cheerfully. "Now I know how to fix this! I just have to think about what someone else wants!"

"Well," Gabe said. "Then I guess I'm going to spend the rest of my life with snow up my nose."

"And I'm going to spend the rest of *mine* in a *tree*!" Britta yelled.

Sparkleton ignored them. "Okay," he said. "Someone has to wish for all the opposite wishes to be fixed. Then I can focus on their happiness and grant that wish."

"I call not it," Zuzu said. The rest of the unicorns all backed away from Sparkleton.

Sparkleton rolled his eyes. "Very funny," he said. Then he frowned thoughtfully. "It should be someone I really, *really* want to help, so it's easy to think about it," he said. He turned to his best friends, Willow and Gabe.

"I think," Sparkleton added, "that it should be someone who has helped me."

Willow pulled her ears back nervously.

Gabe shuffled his hooves.

Sparkleton turned to Nella. The sun was almost set. He had to get this right—there was no time for a second try.

"You gave me a chance to prove myself, Nella," he said. "Now I want to grant *your* wish."

Nella pressed her cheek against Sparkleton's cheek in a unicorn hug.

"Thank you, little brother," she said softly. Then she stepped back and said:

I wish that all of Sparkleton's wishes would be **UNDONE** and that everything in Shimmer Lake would go back to **NORMAL**.

One more chapter to go! Are you feeling SPARKLETASTIC?

11

12

Thy Wish Is Granted

Sparkleton swallowed hard. He was nervous! If he messed this up now, his friends would be stuck with blue tails, white manes, and cloud sandwiches—*forever*.

Nella nodded at him. "You can do this," she said. "I believe in you."

Sparkleton began the spell.

First he stamped his front hooves: left, then right.

Then he lowered his nose to the ground and snorted three times.

Finally, he traced a figure eight in the air with the tip of his horn. It began to glow.

Sparkleton looked into Nella's eyes. *You're my sister and I love you*, he thought. *And I want you to be happy.*

Nella looked back at him. Sparkleton could see that she trusted him. And he knew the wish was going to work.

The little bright place near his heart glowed warmly. Sparkleton shivered all over. This was what magic was *supposed* to feel like.

Thy wish is granted.

And, as the sun set beyond Shimmer Lake, all the opposite wishes vanished.

Gabe shook his head, cloud-free.

Everyone's manes (and Zuzu's tail) went back to normal.

The river of mud disappeared.

And Britta—

"Yaaaaagh!" she screamed as she crashed through the branches of the tree.

Splat! She hit the ground.

"Wow!" Willow said.

"Are you okay?" Dale asked.

Britta popped up. "I'm *fine*," she said, shaking twigs and leaves out of her mane. "No thanks to Sparkleton."

"You're welcome!" Sparkleton said.

"No, I said— Oh, forget it," Britta muttered, and stomped off.

"Well, little brother," Nella said, "have you learned your lesson?"

Sparkleton nodded seriously.

"Yes, I did," he said. "I learned that if I don't listen to my lessons . . ."

"Yes?" Nella said.

"And if I don't think of others . . ." Sparkleton went on.

"Yes?" Nella said.

"I can still *totally* save the day at the last minute," Sparkleton finished. "Me and my awesome friends."

"Sounds about right to me," Willow said. Then she bumped Gabe with her nose until he said, "Fine, me too, I guess."

Sparkleton grinned and knocked horns with his two best friends.

"You're something else, Sparkleton," Nella said.

"I sure am!" Sparkleton agreed.

CONGRATULATIONS!

You've read **12** chapters,

87 pages,

and **5,672** words!

All your **GLITTERRIFIC EFFORT** paid off!

How many
BOOKS
have you read?

What are you
EXCITED
to read next?

Feeling
SHIMMERY?

UNICORN GAMES

THINK!

In the story, I wish to fly. If you could wish for anything in the world, what would it be and why?

FEEL!

Think of a time something you wanted to do went HORRIBLY wrong. How did that make you feel? What were some of the things you tried to do to make it better? Write down your story or tell it to a friend!

ACT!

Think of an important person or unicorn in your life. What are some things you can do to make their day feel a little more GLIMMERIFIC? Draw a picture of your plan!

CALLIOPE GLASS is a writer and editor. She lives in New York City with two small humans and one big human, and a hardworking family of house spiders who are all named Gwen. There are no unicorns in her apartment, but they are always welcome.

HOLLIE MENGERT is an illustrator and animator living in Seattle. She loves drawing animals, making people smile with her work, and spending time with her amazingly supportive family and friends.